THE RUNAWAY BROWNIE

story by Mary Calhoun
pictures by Janet McCaffery

William Morrow & Company 1967

JC

The brownie had been with the family for hundreds of years.

He was their very own brownie, nobody else's.

The folks prized the brownie like a lucky gold piece,

handed down from father to son.

The brownie, though, thought the family belonged to him.

All these years he had looked after the folks

in the stone farmhouse,

there in a misty valley of Scotland.

They called him Angus,

for the name had long been in the family.

Angus was a gruff little creature, half-man, half-beastie.
He had brown curly hair all over his body,
and he wore a brown cloak that came down to his knees.
His pointed ears poked from under his hood,
and his brown wrinkled face was canny and twinky.
His face was canny from knowing things for hundreds of years,
twinky from tricking folk for hundreds of years,
just to make them behave.

And all those years Angus helped the family.
Every night he cleaned the kitchen, hurrying at his work,
muttering, in his scratchy voice,
"Floor scrubbed — ha! Plates washed — hoh!"
Every night he worked in the barn, saying gruffly,
"Corn threshed — ha! Cows milked — hoh!"
In return all he asked was a bowl of cream
and a honeycomb left by the fire. "Supper here – hum!"

In the daytime Angus slept in his own special places—
in a hollow tree nearby, in a cave in the mountain behind,
or in the ruins of a castle high on the crag.
Few folk ever saw him.
The brownie showed himself only once to each master.
Meg, the old woman who cooked in the kitchen,
sometimes saw the tail of his cloak flick through the door.
She respected the brownie for his worth to the family,
and she was careful to put out his supper each night.
And there was a lad who saw the brownie.
The lad was Rob, orphan nephew of the old master.
Rob loved Angus, pawky little brownie
with his shrewd tricks and his faithful ways.
At night Rob watched from half-down the kitchen stairs
as Angus hopped about at his work, grunting,
"Floor scrubbed — ha! Pots washed — hoh! Butter churned — ha!"
Rob wished to join Angus,
yet he knew the creature would only disappear if he did.

So the boy hid his laughing and his longing behind his hands.
But one time Rob crept out to the barn to watch,
and he laughed aloud to see the brownie outwit the hired men,
who'd left extra work for him.
That night the new-gathered hay
was still scattered every which way.

Carefully Angus stacked it in the hayloft.
But last he hid the pitchfork deep under the hay.
By the time the men found it, they'd be sorry
they'd left so much work for the brownie.
Angus chuckled a gruff "Ha!"
and skipped on his way.

Angus heard Rob laugh, too,

but he didn't punish the boy's peeping.

For his canny ears caught the friendship in the laugh.

So Angus worked for the family, and he tricked the family.

But more. He brought good fortune to the family.

The farm prospered, the fields stood thick with barley.

And the household thrived with good cheer.

Now there was one who had never seen the brownie.

But he was waiting, he was waiting.

He was Duncan, grown son of the old master.

And Duncan craved the farm to belong all to him.

He rubbed his hands and waited for the day

when the brownie would show himself to Duncan, the new master.

At last the old father came to the end of his time,

and he died.

"Now!" said Duncan. "Now the farm is mine!

I'll bribe that brownie to bring me

more riches than ever before."

In the kitchen he told old Meg, "Take the finest wool
and make up a braw cloak for Angus, a beautiful cloak and hood.
Tomorrow he will show himself to me,
and he shall have a grand gift from his new master."
The old woman threw up her hands.
"Don't give Angus a cloak!" she cried.

No brownie will take a rich gift, she told him.

Brownies have nothing but scorn for bribes.

"Our brownie will take insult at the gift

and leave us forever," warned Meg.

On the stairs Rob listened and trembled at what might happen.

Duncan only laughed.

"A new cloak and hood will make Angus love me.
Now do as I say!"
And he ordered Meg to set out a feast
for the brownie that night —
a bucket of cream, a haunch of mutton, and a fine big cake.
Meg muttered and cried, but she did.
For Duncan was the new master.
She made up the cloak, and she set out the feast.
And when she went to bed, Rob hid all the food.
He loved the pawky brownie,
and he feared the feast-bribe would drive him away.
But there was nothing Rob could do about the cloak.
Duncan had taken it.

Next day the brownie came to the parlor
and showed himself to Duncan.

"You are my master. I am your brownie," said Angus.

Duncan grinned. "I hope you liked your feast," he said.

"Now here is a fine cloak
for a good brownie who will bring me riches."

Angus took the cloak, looked at it,

and all the twinkiness went out of his face.

He threw the cloak on the floor and stamped on it.

"A new cloak and a new hood!" he growled.

"Your brownie will do no more good!"

And he fled out of the house in a rage.

Rob, listening at the door, cried, "Stop, Angus!"

But the brownie vanished from sight.

Meg crouched in the kitchen and wailed.

Duncan only laughed and said, "He'll be back."

Every night Rob put out the brownie's cream by the fire,

but old Meg told him the food would do no good,

and she was right.

The cream was never eaten.

Every night the lad grieved on the stairs,

waiting for the brownie who didn't come.

Then things went badly for the farm.

The barley died in the fields. The cows gave thin milk.

The hired men quarreled and left the farm.

A mist hung over the valley, and gloom hung over the family.

Duncan stormed in the parlor.

"I'm a poor man, since the brownie left.

I'll find Angus and make him come back!"
He went through the mist to the hollow oak tree,
where the brownie was known to sleep.
Down in the trunk he saw a curled-up shape with points of ears.
Duncan shouted down the hollow,

"Come out of there, Angus! Come home, I order you!"
The shape stirred, the pointed ears flicked.
In anger came the voice from the hollow,
"Nay! Angus serves you no more!"
And things grew worse on the farm.

Old Meg wailed in the kitchen,

for the family was doomed, if the brownie didn't come back.

At last she went through the mist to plead with the brownie.

She looked in the tree, but he wasn't there.

Meg toiled her way up the mountain to the cave.

Back in the black hole

she saw a curled-up shape with points of ears.

"Come back to the farm, Angus," she begged.

"Come home for the sake of the family."

The shape stirred, the pointed ears flicked.

"Nay!" came the gruff voice in the cave.

"Duncan is not my master."

And so the old woman had to tell Duncan,

"The brownie will never come back to serve you."

"Then I'll stay here no longer!" raged the selfish master.

"This poor farm is nothing to me, if it won't bring me riches.

I'll go to the city to seek my fortune."

Meg cried and begged and shamed him for leaving the farm
that had belonged to his family for hundreds of years.
Yet Duncan brushed her aside.
He got on his horse and rode away forever,
pushed on by his greed for riches.

Then Rob, his face grieved thin, went out through the mist
to look for Angus.
He looked in the tree, no brownie there.
He looked in the cave, no brownie there.
The boy climbed on, with the heather scratching his legs.

High up to the mountain crag climbed Rob.
There in the drifting mist, on a wall of castle ruins,
he saw the shape of a brownie and points of ears.
Not a curled-up shape, but Rob's pawky brownie,
hopping and whirling on the stone wall.
"Come home to us, Angus," Rob called.
"Come home, for I miss you."
Then the mist swirled away,
and the sun shone over the green mountain.
And the brownie on the castle wall
showed himself to Rob.
"I will," said Angus, "because you want me.

Now Duncan is gone, you are my new master."
"Ah, Angus!" cried Rob with gladness to his friend.

Then the boy and the brownie
ran down the mountain through the heather.

Rob laughed,

and the small brownie's face was twinky again

as he said gruffly, "Floor to scrub — ha!

Barn to clean — hoh! Cows to milk — ha!"

From that day on, the farm prospered.

The fields stood thick with barley,

the cows gave rich milk,

old Meg sang in the kitchen.

And Angus served his master

for all of Rob's long, happy life.

AUTHOR'S NOTES

The brownie of Scotch folklore seems to be something of an ancestral spirit presiding over the fortunes of a family. Of course, helpful house elves appear in the folklore of many European countries, and a farmer often wished to acquire an elf to serve the household and bring good luck. Scotch tales, however, show the brownie as a family's own personal elf, inherited from generation to generation. Some students of folklore suggest brownies may be remnants of an aboriginal race of very short men. The folklorists theorize that brownie tales arose from peasants' beliefs that the spirits of desirable ancestors stayed with the families.

The brownie was a creature of impeccable virtue, ready to do his share of work, and shocked at bribery or flattery. If offered a special gift of a cloak or new shoes, he would leave the farm in a huff, perhaps never to return. Not always a house dweller, he was sometimes called "the little old man of the barn," sometimes said to live in ruined castles near the families he served.

My story is woven from fragmentary tales mostly from the southwest of Scotland, the districts of Wigtown, Kirkcudbright, and Dumfries. My principal sources are *The Fairy Mythology* by Thomas Keightley and *Fairy Tradition in Britain* by Lewis Spence.